Hal plays Hide and Seek

Om KIDZ
An imprint of Om Books International

Om Kidz | Om Books International

Reprinted in 2023

Corporate & Editorial Office
A-12, Sector 64, Noida 201 301
Uttar Pradesh, India
Phone: +91 120 477 4100
Email: editorial@ombooks.com
Website: www.ombooksinternational.com

ISBN: 978-93-52760-26-8

Printed in India

10 9 8 7 6 5 4 3 2

Sales Office
107, Ansari Road, Darya Ganj
New Delhi 110 002, India
Phone: +91 11 4000 9000
Email: sales@ombooks.com
Website: www.ombooks.com

Hal plays Hide and Seek

Paste your photograph here

My name is

____

Hal is a **happy** little boy.
He lives in a big **house**
on a **high hill**.

The **house has** a big **hall**. **Hal** runs and plays games in the **hall**.

There is a **huge** barn behind **Hal's house**. The barn is **home** to many animals.

There are **hens** and **horses** in the barn. It also **has** a lot of **hay**.

Today is a **holiday**. **Hal** is in **his house**. **His** friend **Holly** comes to play.

“**Hello, Holly**,” says **Hal**.

“Shall we play **hide**-and-seek?”

It is **Hal's** turn to **hide**.

He hurries into the barn.

He hides under the **hay**.

It is **hot** inside.

Hal hopes that **Holly** does not find **him.** **He** makes a **hole** in the **hay** to look outside.

Hal waits for **Holly**,
but nothing **happens**.
All of a sudden, a **huge**
shadow falls over **him**.

Hal is afraid. **He** thinks it is a **hairy** monster. **He** tries to move away, but it is **hard** to move with the **hay** on **him**.

Hal feels a **hand** on **him**.

Hal screams for **help**.

"I got you," says **Holly**.

"**Here** you are!"

Hal's heart is **hammering** loudly.

But there is no monster in the barn.

It is only **Holly** wearing a riding **hat**!

Holly thinks **Hal** is **hurt**.

But **he** is only afraid.

She **helps Hal** to **his** feet.

He is **heavy**!

Holly hugs Hal. He feels better. They play for **half** an **hour**. Soon they are **hungry**. They **head home** to **have** dinner.

Know your words

Naming words

Hal hens hole
house horses hand
hill hay heart
hall holiday hat
home Holly head

Describing words

happy high hairy
heavy huge hard
hungry hot half

Doing words

has happens hug
holds help hopes
hide hammering
hurries hurt

Sight words

he him hour
his here have

Circle the things hidden in the barn. The clue-box below will help you.

Clue-box: Hen, Hat, Horse, Hammer, Hand, Head

Join the dots and colour the image to show what Holly is wearing.

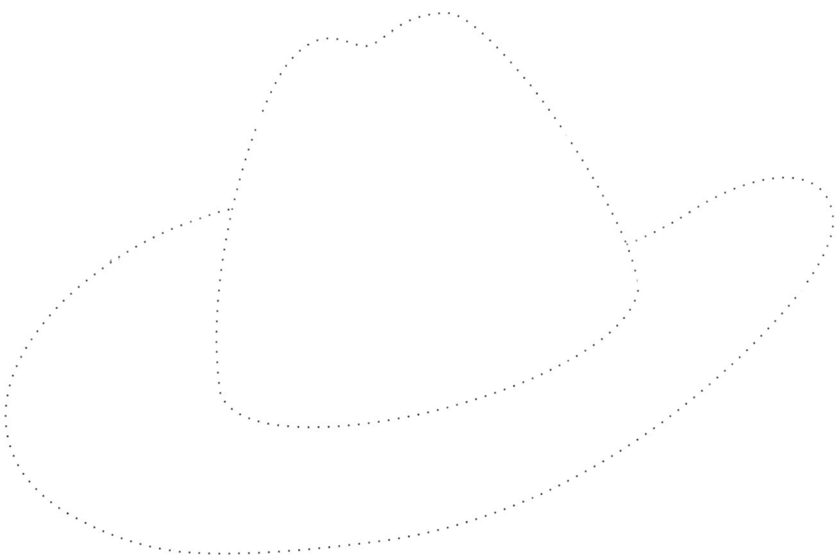

Circle the words that begin with 'H'.

hat

barn

hay

game

horse

little

hen

feet

help